M.A. Murad

A NEW PROPHET

AUSTIN MACAULEY PUBLISHERS™

LONDON • CAMBRIDGE • NEW YORK • SHARJAH

A CIP catalogue record for this title is available from the British Library.

ISBN 9781035824373 (Paperback)
ISBN 9781035824380 (ePub e-book)

www.austinmacauley.com

First Published 2024
Austin Macauley Publishers Ltd®
1 Canada Square
Canary Wharf
London
E14 5AA

20240709

The cover art and the illustrations in this book are reproduced from original water colors by the author.

You can contact the author at
https://mamurad.ampbk.com

*Al **Muntazara;** the long-awaited one. The one whose homecoming has become a myth to the folk of Herta. The woman who left when she was only eighteen has finally returned. After fifty years of wandering, she came back with naught but the clothes that covered her slender body and the star-shaped birthmark on the palm of her right hand.*

When she left from the harbour of Herta all those years ago, it was from a flimsy wooden pier that rocked more than the boats that were moored to it. Now, at the same place, she stepped onto a concrete one with only large ships docked at it. The new pier felt cold under her bare feet and less trustworthy than the old wooden one.

"The last of my journeys brings me back to where it all began; Herta, the fishing village of my birth, childhood, and adolescence. The land

of my ancestors. Yet, as I crave to fill my yearning lungs, its air resembles nothing of the one that filled them afore I left. The lighthouse I know well, and the name written atop the harbour master's house tells me that I have returned to a familiar place. My soul, however, feels estranged still."

Where once there was an open meadow leading up from the harbour to the hills, many streets she presently had to cross, and many buildings shaded the earth that the trees once did.

As she reached the hilltop, she saw that the village she had left when she was but a young woman, had become a big town intent on becoming a city soon.

She descended the hill and walked through the streets that she no longer recognised. She had a painful longing to return to the house of her birth.

There were many people in cars and on buses. Very few walked on the sidewalks or sat on benches, and most of those who did, were staring down at or talking over some device to people who were not there with them. She was certain that not a single one of them caught a glimpse of her.

"What germ has infected my people? Where are the salutations that addressed people by their names? Who stole from them the nods of acknowledgement and the courteous handshakes and smiles? Where are the children and where are their street games? Can no one see this barefoot person in foreign garb? Have I become invisible or have the passersby gone blind?"

In her mind's eye, she saw where her home was, and she followed her heart towards it, walking around buildings that were built in her absence and through alleys that were not there before.

In front of her, at last, she saw her family's old house; derelict and long abandoned, it looked like a faded picture of old or an incomplete artist's sketch. The door and the windows were boarded up and its once bright white coat was gone. The trees she climbed on as a child stood leafless and dead; like faithful ghosts guarding the memories of long ago.

It was at its door that she sat cross-legged. She spread her arms and rested her hands on her knees. With her eyes closed, she turned her hands upwards towards the sky. On the palm of her right hand was the birthmark in the shape of a star.

Three days and three nights had passed, before she turned her hands down and clasped her knees. She took a deep breath and opened her eyes.

Leading to where she sat, and in every direction, the streets and alleys were overflown with people. Some were standing on their feet, while others were sitting on chairs or on rugs they brought from their homes.

There were people at every window and on every roof of each building from where she could be seen. The quiet was the defining feature of the scene.

An old person stepped forward from the crowd and pointed to a spread that had been laid before the Prophet. She looked and saw an abundance of offerings; fruits and breads of every kind, cheeses and wines, folded new clothes, and several pairs of new shoes. The

Prophet found that sometime earlier, someone had placed a blanket on her slender shoulders.

The old person then said, "The young did not know who you were, but the old remember the person who left Herta all those years ago; the girl with a star-shaped sign on her palm. The young of this town have only seen you and heard you through the new media, but have never believed us, old folk, when we told them that you, the Prophet, were born and raised here in Herta. Now they flock to see for themselves that it is, in fact, you; the person who one day left and never returned."

He paused as he looked at the crowd, then said, "But now, at last, you are back. Your family has long gone, and their name, like yours, has been forgotten. However, I and the elders always believed in our hearts that you would one day return. To us, you have been Al Muntazara."

He then looked at the house behind her and said, "Certain that someday you would come back, the elders made sure that your house was never to be demolished or occupied. Tomorrow we shall start renovating it to befit a Prophet."

From the wide selection of foods in front of her, the Prophet picked up an apple and ate it in silence as everyone looked on. She ate the apple, then buried the apple's core with its seeds in the soil.

She said: "Take this food and these clothes to the poor who need them, for as much as I appreciate your generosity, I have no need for all this. And I certainly do not need to drink water from a plastic bottle."

Her voice was serene and level, yet it reached everyone in the crowd, and they began removing the food and clothes they had brought earlier.

The crowd made way for a shopkeeper who brought her a glass and a jug of water, and she smiled at him, poured some water on the earth where she buried the apple seeds, then drank some herself.

She turned to the old man with affection and said: "I am but a visitor to this town and to this life. The earth shall be my bed and the sky my blanket. Winds shall be the walls to surround me. For me, my friend, that would be a home worthy of a Prophet."

When all the food and clothes were taken away, she took another sip of water and closed her eyes. She stretched her arms with her palms turned to the sky and breathed the silence of the crowd in.

After a few moments, the Prophet opened her eyes, removed the blanket from her shoulders, and slowly stood up.

People gasped as they saw that her white hair, like a silver waterfall, cascaded all the way down past the back of her knees.

She looked at the crowd and said, "People of Herta. People of now and people of before and of later. Here is where I end my days, though it is not here that I die. You have come to see me and to hear my words, and I embrace you all and hold you to my bosom as if each were a sibling or a child of mine.

When I speak to you, it is the entire world that I am speaking to. My love for life, this earth, and all its creatures is the blood that will run warm through my veins until I depart on my final journey. A resilient love that gave me the strength to persevere in my search for the Truth.

Yet, if my time-weathered face makes me appear older than some who preceded me by birth, and if my wisdom is that of a person who has lived a thousand years, and if my body is as tired as someone's who has quarried the mountains of the world, that my beloved, is because of the weight of the anguish I bear for the injustices I have witnessed people inflict upon earth, upon other people, and upon fellow creatures in the places I have travelled to.

You have seen me and have heard my words through various forms of media. Today, however, I have come in person to offer you a gift that I have dedicated my entire life to crafting. It is a gift born out of an insight that I gained from understanding nature, from sharing experiences and listening to storytellers, from holding the hand of a child on its first steps and that of a dying grandparent, and from walking alongside factory workers and farmers, miners and traders, teachers and students.

Brothers and sisters, children of this world, ask me and I shall not withhold the knowledge

I have acquired. But I urge you not to simply write down or record my words on paper or in your devices, for you risk becoming enslaved by your notebooks and screens while my image is repeatedly replayed over the years to come.

Instead, I implore you to truly "feel" what I say, lest your memory betray you in the future.

I beseech your inner selves to open up to my words like a flower would to sunlight."

Aylana, a person of similar age to the Prophet's, raised her hand and said, "Speak to us of Love."

The Prophet replied: "Love is the noblest of feelings. It is the cloak in which everything becomes beautiful for both the lover and the beloved.

Love triggers empathy and kindness, softening even the hardest of hearts. It unveils new meanings in things we thought we knew well.

Love inspires ordinary people to become poets and musicians, painters and sculptors, builders and revolutionaries.

Love fosters selflessness and finds ways to give, even when there are hardly any means to do so.

No matter how resistant your heart may be, Love shall break down its doors and windows. It will consume you entirely and hold you until you surrender to its tender embrace. In that surrender, you shall become a better person, discovering your truer self.

However, Love itself is an insatiable being. It constantly demands to be fed and craves its favourite sustenance: Respect and Trust.

Lovers must continuously remind each other of their devotion; offering praise to their beloved. Even the smallest of smiles can reignite the embers of those early moments when Love first blossomed.

If, however, Love's hunger remains unsatisfied, it transforms into a beast that devours warmth and happy memories. Unfed Love poisons the present and the future with potions brewed from jealousy and mistrust. Hungry Love magnifies the tiniest of faults, draining the mind of beauty and compassion. It consumes both; the lovers and itself.

When you fall in Love, celebrate that fall by surrendering completely to its power. Then, open your heart to love everyone and everything around you. In doing so, Love will be fortified, and it will fortify you in return.

It is only then that the loss of Love becomes unbearable.

In Love's strength, you will discover your own strength. You will understand the true meaning of tolerance and understanding, you will learn patience and sacrifice, and finally grasp the essence of your own being.

If, one day, and through no fault of your beloved, you find yourself falling out of love with them, then you never truly loved them. You may have mistaken the feeling of being in love for love itself. On that forsaken day, go and tell them the truth. Concealing your honest feelings and keeping them invested in a Love that you know is not genuine would be less compassionate than setting them free to seek Love elsewhere.

When you embark on a search for Love, take your time. Be patient and be vigilant. Look for it with a keen heart rather than keen eyes. And if you grow weary, questioning your pursuit, and just when you are on the verge of returning home empty-handed, Love shall be there as you turn your face; for Love will always find those who seek it."

While looking lovingly at a sleeping baby in her arms, Nita said, "Tell us about Children."

"Children are the embodiment of your instinct for preservation. They are your successors and your contribution to humanity, but they should not be treated as mere extensions to your unfinished stories.

This I say, because living vicariously through your children confines them to a world of your dreams, not theirs. Seek not to fulfil your own aspirations through them, for they will have their own to pursue and fulfil. Treat them with the dignity of the autonomous stars that they are, rather than satellites.

Teach them to make their own choices from an early age, lest they become mere followers in their minds and souls. Show them that there are paths different from the ones that you know or have taken. Teach them that knowledge and empathy are the surest ways to navigate these paths.

Do not judge them, nor encourage them to judge others, for judgment breeds hostility and fuels prejudice.

Treat them with respect, and they will grow up to be respectful individuals.

Plant trees with them, and they will grow up valuing the planet.

Help the needy with them, and they will grow up to be giving and compassionate.

Teach them, and learn from them, but not once should you force your beliefs upon them.

Let them choose their own path, with you walking not ahead of them or beside them, but right behind them until they need you no more.

When they eventually go their own way, do not lament the empty nest they leave behind. Instead, rejoice in their freedom and the new nests they will create for themselves one day."

*The old person who first spoke to the Prophet, then said, "I am **Sole**, and as someone who has lived in Herta all his life, without once setting foot beyond its hills and shores, I ask you to talk to us about the people of the world and how different they are from us."*

The Prophet said: "As I speak to you now, there are those who are busy translating my words into tens and hundreds of beautiful tongues for countless eager listeners and viewers around the world. When a melody is played and a person hears it, that person's skin colour or mother tongue cannot change the truth carried by the melody's notes, nor can that person's beliefs or politics.

People in various places are, in truth, not as different from you or other people as you might perceive. I have been with people who do not resemble you in their appearance, nor do they speak your language.

I have visited people who worship more gods than you do, and others who worship fewer. There were people who dressed differently from you and others who saw no need to cover their bodies. None of those differences could conceal the basic beauty of their humanity.

I have shared meals with people where the food was served on a banana leaf and with others from a golden bowl, but what mattered most was who I shared that food with; a piece of stale bread tastes sweeter than nectar when it is shared with a person who views me as an equal; as a fellow human being."

Sole then asked, "But are all people equal, though?"

The Prophet replied: "Do not all people possess dreams and aspirations? Do they not desire to see their children grow up in good health and in good company? Do they not all want to live in dignity and peace? The dreams you share with other human beings transcend the superficial and apparent differences you have with them.

Everything you shall hear me say revolves around "Love"; it is from Love that the bonds tying you to your humanity and to one another sprout.

If you love your sons and daughters, do not oppress or humiliate someone else's. And if you honour and respect your parents, then honour and respect everyone else's. That is how people become equal.

Kindness and respect do not know colour or creed. Laughter and tears are the same in any culture and are shared by all tongues and beliefs. Pain and relief do not care how much money one has or what colour their skin is. Sickness and health, and the changing seasons of the year are blind to your differences. That is why people are equal.

If you expand your circle of love, one ring at a time, it will grow until there is no room for greed or bigotry. Like a single droplet falling on a pond, its ripples expand and chase the dirt and dead leaves from the surface of the water, casting them ashore. Start such a ripple today and every day.

Know your neighbour and your fellow worker better. See if they need something you can offer in their time of need, and they will remember you in your time of need. That is how people become equal.

You are all descendants of this earth, and had no choice as to when and where you were born, to which parents, the colour of your skins, or your genders. None of these should be viewed as achievements or privileges, nor should they be carried as a burden for which one must pay. And that is why people should be equal."

Amoni then asked the Prophet about men and women and if they should be treated as equals.

The Prophet smiled and said: "There was a time when women were not considered to be as wise or as strong as men.

Yet, here you all are, standing before an aged woman seeking her wisdom, and feeding off her strength. The times have certainly changed, but perhaps not enough.

The equality you seek is, in reality, a fairness in treatment, and the root of inequality lies in the unfair expectations placed upon either.

From early childhood, boys and girls are instructed in what is expected of them as they grow up, and are taught about their future roles in society.

There are more things that women can do and men cannot than the things that men can do and women cannot. Yet, you have been made to believe otherwise.

A man and a woman journey through life in an interdependent existence. Neither can, nor should, seek an alternative way; each contributes a crucial part that complements and completes the other's.

For the relationship between men and women to be fair, neither should be paid more than the other for taking on the same burdens, and neither should be subjugated by the other when the burdens vary."

Amoni then said, "Tell us how you view sexuality and sexual relations." Upon hearing this, some of the parents started walking away with their children. The Prophet urged them to stay, saying: "Stay, brothers and sisters, and let your young ones stay! Are they not the celebration of your union?" The parents stayed with their children.

The Prophet continued: "Nothing could be more beautiful than the meeting of lovers in a bodily union. It is a union that awakens their consciousness and unleashes their hidden sensations and yearnings.

It is their bodies surrendering to the fantasies of their minds. It is, at once, the desire and the satisfaction of being desired.

Sexual urges are embodied in your natural instincts. They guide a significant portion of your life and shape much of your behaviour. Unlike other creatures, humans have evolved to take their sexual desire beyond the purpose of procreation or dominance. Your sexual drive is not solely awakened by the seasons of the year or the safety of numbers.

And Oh, how elevated is the gratification when the merging of bodies brings an amalgamation of the souls into one!

It is then like a musical duo playing in perfect harmony. The universe is then bewitched by their two instruments, as the music seeps through the interstice between their skins.

You ask me, and I say that sex is sublime and beyond reproach when driven by consensual love! If two adults are consenting, then you should not concern yourselves with how they derive satisfaction for their longing.

Who is to say what your heart should hunger for? Who can shame your sexual desires while defending and boasting their own?

Yes, my dear Amoni, nothing is deviant or criminal if the people involved are consenting adults.

Having said that, you should always keep your sexual affairs to yourselves, lest others, in their rigid minds, find ways to judge, label, or even persecute you."

Albin asked the Prophet to speak of Friendship, and the Prophet replied: "Friendship transcends all other relationships, surpassing even those of marriage or companionship. It is a connection that goes beyond kinship and runs deeper than any other bond.

Friendship is the repository of your joys and sorrows, and of strengths and weaknesses. It is the vault where your secrets are held in trust.

Do not think of your friend as someone you can wrong and expect forgiveness, but rather, as someone who can wrong you and be forgiven by you.

Your friend is the one with whom your soul can stand naked, without feeling vulnerable or ashamed.

Your friend is one who will cry with you and cry for you. Your friend will laugh with you and laugh for you, but never at you.

Your wealth in friends is determined by the richness of their Friendships and not by their number.

Most of the time, having only one true friend can fill your life with more than many acquaintances, companions, or family members ever could.

When lovers, siblings, or parents and their children become friends, then Friendship reaches an unparalleled level.

True Friendship goes beyond blood ties and merges with the depth of your soul. You will sense it with every breath and each heartbeat.

A true friend may be separated from you by years and vast distances, but when you reunite, everything between you resumes as if you were never apart, and you pick up from where you left all that time ago.

Do not blame your friends for not inquiring about you, for you should know that it is in their soul that you dwell, as it is in yours that they do. You have laid your soul at their feet, and they have done the same for you."

Why are you dressed like that? Is that how we are supposed to dress?" asked **Mirean**, a young dressmaker.

The Prophet glanced down at her own attire; a long shirt and a pair of worn-out jeans, her feet bare.

She then said: "You begin your lives naked. Whether born to beggars, or to kings and queens. That is the briefest moment of genuine equality that humans experience during their time on this earth.

Indeed, all humans once roamed naked, and when they covered their bodies, it was to protect themselves against the elements.

However, egotism took hold, leading traders and their partners to believe they should dress differently from those who fished, ploughed, or engaged in any labour that made them sweat. Clothing became a tool for differentiation.

Yet, I pity those who perceive themselves as inferior due to their modest attire, or those who consider themselves superior simply because they are clad in silk. Should they not recognise that the toil of the former is what produces the cotton, wool, silk, and leather that the latter flaunt?

Clothiers are well aware of the fickleness and vanity of people. They lay traps for the unsuspecting; dictating trends that people blindly follow.

They will tell you that one trend is out and another is in, prompting you to hastily discard the old and acquire the new, willingly surrendering your hard-earned money and becoming slaves to fashion and their brand.

Unbeknownst to many who are slaves to fashion, the clothiers have a system that enslaves the laborers who create the garments as well.

It is not uncommon for those who sell you branded clothing to exploit impoverished individuals, including children, in the making of your clothes. Those workers toil day and night to make clothes that many of them cannot afford to wear. In return for their work, they receive barely enough to feed themselves or their families, while their employers amass fortunes."

"Do we then have to make our own clothes? Are the clothes you are wearing not also bought?" inquired Mirean.

"If you possess the skills to make your own clothes, then you should do so.

However, if you choose to buy them, do so mindfully and for your comfort.

Avoid getting caught in the snares laid out for you on billboards and in various media.

Do not dress to imitate others or to stand out, rather, dress how your body feels the seasons and dress clean and in comfort.

Look after your clothes and think of the person you might pass them on to.

What you are not told is that clothes can, and should, be shared. A sister from years ago gifted me these pants I am wearing, and a brother provided the shirt on my back.

It is undeniable that you need clothes, but if only people realised the amount of resources expended and pollution generated in their making, they would strive to make them last and take pride in sharing and reusing them.

Mend torn garments, alter, tighten, widen, embellish, and upcycle until only rags for cleaning are all that remain.

Be conscious of the impact your clothing choices have on both the environment and the lives of those who toil to create them."

Zira, the lutanist, stood up and addressed the Prophet saying, "Talk to us about Music!"

With her eyes closed, and a smile on her lips, the prophet paused for a moment as if she was listening to a melody playing in her head, before saying: "Music is the language of your inner muse. It resides deep within your subconscious, and fills the spaces of your forgetfulness.

I have heard people who have never listened to Music before, humming melodies that are unfamiliar to others or to themselves even.

Music possesses the power to soothe you, or propel you forward, to evoke feelings of joy or of melancholy, and to focus your thoughts or distract them.

All that it can do and more because its origin lies within your very essence. Its earliest manifestation emerged through your imitation of life and nature.

Wasn't the loving beat of your mother's heart the first rhythm that timed your life as it started in her womb?

The melodies of birdsongs inspired the creation of flutes and violins, the gentle patter of raindrops on a lake gave birth to the lute and lyre, and the mighty roar of thunder became the sound of the kettledrum. When all of nature's sounds intertwine, they perform the sweet symphony of life itself.

Musicians have the power to manipulate your hearts and souls through Music's impeccable structure and its resonances.

Still, in moments of silence, when you find yourself enveloped in stillness, you will hear the distant echoes of your childhood. You will hear songs you have long forgotten coming back to you. Your minds conjure up melodies; it is the universe whispering its secrets to you when all goes quiet.

If you cannot teach your children to play an instrument, then instil in them a love and *appreciation for music. For Music has the power to order the mind and inspire the soul."*

Voldar then asked the Prophet about the other arts and the artists.

The Prophet replied: "Art is the realisation of your ideas, brought to life on the pages of a book, the surface of a canvas, through sculpture, or in the assembly of stones as architects erect monuments.

It is through Art that your creativity finds its unique expression, setting you apart from other species.

Art provides an outlet for artists to express themselves when other means fail them.

Art enables the imagination to explore realms that are mysterious to conscious thought, and it returns with things of wonder from those realms.

Through Art, an artist can transcend the limitations of the physical world. The artist can also make the abstract tangible, giving *form to myths, folklore, and beliefs that can only be grasped through writings, paintings, carvings, music, or architecture.*

Art is the guardian of human growth. It is through Art that you are able to understand history and ensure the continuity of human civilisation.

Artists find fulfilment in their creative endeavours while serving humanity. It is through Art that their souls are liberated to creatively capture the spirit of the times in their works. From writing to painting, from sculpting to architecture, every Art form originates from a simple muse that evolves into a profound testimony to the creative existence of humans.”

Kamida, the learned, asked the Prophet about her thoughts on Teaching and Learning.

"Oh, ever-curious Kamida. As you once taught me in my youth and now seek my wisdom, you must recognise that Teaching and Learning are intertwined.

May I repay some of what I owe you, learned Kamida, by saying that education is everything. Books, classes, tests, and academic certificates are merely tools; they should not be seen as ends in themselves. What you should strive to instil in the eager minds of the young is a love for knowledge and the skills needed to navigate the challenges that life may present.

From an early age, ignite their curiosity about the world around them.

The universe is a never-ending source of understanding and learning. Teach them to engage their senses; to watch, listen, smell, taste, and touch; for these experiences cannot be adequately captured in words or taught in a classroom.

You will do well to remember that not all people will derive the same lessons from these experiences; different individuals will learn different things from observing the same phenomenon.

Embrace those differences and share them. Enrich their minds with the beauty of science and of myth. Then sit back and contemplate the new lessons that you have learnt from your pupils.

Do not impose your own predetermined path upon them. Instead, show them the vast array of possibilities and provide them with the means to explore.

Let them follow their passions, for it is through pursuing what brings them joy that they may find their true fortune.

Even if you believe that their choice of doing something they enjoy might not bring them fortune in their future, remember that it is always better to be unfortunately happy than fortunately miserable.

As the young learn from you, they can also teach you. Future ideas dwell within their young and fresh understanding, and their eyes are the beacon that illuminates the path ahead. It is their youthful ideas that shall prevail when yours become old and irrelevant.

Knowledge is an armour that protects people when darkness falls; the educated become torchbearers, while the ignorant stumble blindly."

Mahad asked the Prophet about finding contentment and accepting one's place in the world.

The Prophet replied: "My dear young Mahad, I have heard wise people tell inquirers: "Just be yourself." To the inquirers I say: Nay, do not merely be yourself, but strive to be the best version of yourself that you can be.

Look not to others and wish to be like them, for you cannot truly know what pains lay hidden beneath the surface that you admire.

Like a stream of water through the valleys, your life shall flow. Turning around hurdles or removing them from its path. Other streams may join yours, forming a mighty river.

Along the way, that river will face boulders and fallen trees that may slow or even stop its flow. When that happens, and when it may seem that the river's journey has ended, the water patiently rises, until one day, it bursts through with more force and determined destination.

Set your goals as high as your curiosity allows, but ensure they are achievable; for a stream will never flow uphill.

Behind closed eyes, a painter envisions a painting telling a timeless tale. On a canvass that has no boundaries, the colours appear to blend flawlessly, and light and shade seem to be as if bestowed by a heavenly sensibility; the painter's vision is immeasurable.

With eyes open, the artist is dispirited to see that the canvas is restricted by the size of its frame, and that the colours do not blend on the pallet as well as was envisioned.

From the first brush stroke and until the painting is completed, tangibility makes the artwork limited; it, at once, becomes measurable.

Know in your heart that what you aspire to will always exceed what you ultimately achieve. I do not ask you to ground your dreams; rather, I urge you to dream boldly and persistently, never surrendering or being discouraged by the limitations of reality, and embracing the infinite vastness of your imagination.

When you reflect upon your life's journey, may you find contentment in the pursuit of your passions, knowing that you have made a difference in the lives of others and left a lasting legacy behind."

Beltar, *the scientist, then asked the Prophet about Technology and its impact on the future of humanity.*

The Prophet said: "Unlike some prophets, I do not possess the ability to foresee the future, nor do I have powers of divination. However, through my perception and the experiences I have gained on my journeys, I have developed an understanding that comes from my openness to learn from my surroundings, and from every fellow human being I encounter.

I believe that Technology, much like art, is a reflection of evolution and human progress. It should be embraced for the positive contributions it can bring to humanity. Consider the countless lives saved by the progress in medicine, and the convenience of efficient transportation.

How many sweet songs, wonderful books, and beautiful paintings would have been lost, or remained unknown to you had there not been the Technology to record and print them? How many people from distant lands would have remained foreign to you had the camera and telephone not been invented?

Today, however, I encounter people who are so engrossed in their technological devices that they fail to notice the world around them. Their focus has shifted from the vastness of the horizon to the confines of small screens.

It grieves me to see people installing screensavers of the sky or the ocean on their devices instead of raising their eyes to witness them in their full glory.

It saddens me to see that search engines have replaced libraries and that books have been substituted by computers.

It used to be that when you chose a book to read, you did so out of genuine interest in the subject or its author. Turning a few pages could not lead you to news, fashion trends, or celebrity gossip. Books offered a focused and immersive experience.

While you now have access to an abundance of information at a faster pace, you are also creating a generation of distracted and impatient individuals.

Nowadays, children are expected to develop their minds and their social skills through digital communication from behind screens in the confines of their rooms, without them ever needing to physically interact with others.

While I acknowledge the convenience of online shopping, research, and virtual gaming, I, as a romantic and a realist, insist that interacting with the shopkeeper, the manufacturer and the farmer cannot be replaced by buying their products and services online.

Interacting with shopkeepers, manufacturers, and farmers in person holds a value that goes beyond mere transactions. There is a richness in face-to-face communication and the connections you build with others in your communities.

Similarly, engaging in real physical activities like playing on swings, building treehouses, and participating in outdoor games with real friends holds a depth of experience that virtual gaming cannot replicate.

The rapid pace at which technological changes are occurring is unnatural. When climbing a mountain, climbers find level spots at various intervals to rest and reflect on their progress before planning their next steps.

These pauses are crucial for understanding the challenges that lie ahead, and recalibrating one's approach. However, in the realm of Technology, there seems to be no such respite. People are constantly pushed forward without a chance to ponder the essence of their pursuits, and without a clear destination.

While I cannot predict the future, I have a premonition of humanity being diminished by the dependence on the virtual. I fear a world where music is composed by non-musicians, books authored by non-writers, and visual art is created by non-artists.

There is a danger in racing to teach machines to perform tasks that skilled individuals were once proficient in. When those individuals are no longer present, you will be left with machines that can perform only the last task they were taught. More dangerous still, is if the machines start teaching themselves and improving their performance without your help.

On that day, your achievements will be dwarfed next to theirs, and you will stand wondering how it all went wrong.

If you view Technology as a tool to enhance your capabilities rather than replace them, then you can pursue its advancement with open minds and hearts. However, you must remain cautious of those who seek to exploit Technology for their own gains, using it to manipulate your thoughts and invade your privacy."

"Prophet sister, tell us of Time," said **Sepet**, the clockmaker.

"Time is subjective, my dear Sepet. It holds different meanings for different individuals. To the young, Time can feel slow, as they eagerly await the opportunity to do things beyond their current capabilities. They see Time as an obstacle standing between them and their aspirations. However, as one grows older and takes on more responsibilities, Time seems to speed up; it feels that days have shorter hours, months have fewer days, and that there are not enough years in a lifetime.

When you long for something, Time becomes a burden. Yet, when you dread another, it pulls you closer with frightening speed. In both instances, anxiety skews your understanding of Time, making it appear different than it truly is.

Time is a cushion that absorbs the pains of the past. It has the power to change perceptions and ideas.

Having said that, Time itself remains constant. As long as the planets and their moons continue their cycles, Time will faithfully tick forward as it always has.

But my dear Sepet, the question you should ask is not about Time itself, but rather, what to do with the Time you have. To that I say: give ample time to the things that truly matter most to you and your fellow humans, and spare little or no time for things that hold no significance.

Take the time to understand yourself. Meditate on your desires, contemplate your abilities, and acknowledge your weaknesses.

Make time for your loved ones, for you do not know how long you will have them around for.

If you engage in a creative endeavour, take the necessary time to craft it well. Haste may lead to delays in corrections or the need to start anew.

Above all, brothers and sisters, take the time to appreciate beauty. Remember that sometimes, true beauty lies beyond the surface of things that you may take for granted. Even seemingly mundane objects can hold hidden wonders if you take the time to explore them.

Time wasted dwelling on the past is time squandered. Instead, use Time to plan the remainder of your journey and should you deviate on your path, make sure to make any of those deviations rewarding and nourishing to your spirit."

"What and how should we eat?" asked **Monag** the cook.

"Eat what you need and eat what you plant. Eat in season and eat in moderation. Eat when you are hungry, but do not eat till you are full.

The world is a plentiful garden, filled with delicious and nutritious offerings. It is sorrowful to witness food being wasted while many people suffer from hunger, or that excessive production goes unshared.

Your desire for quantity and variety has allowed opportunists to manipulate your food. They create unnatural strains and inject animals with artificial hormones. And you buy more and more from them, and they reap more and more from you.

The rich have convinced the poor that it is cheaper to import their food rather than grow it themselves.

While this may have been true at some stage, the poor have since lost the skills and the lands necessary for farming. They have become dependent on the rich, who control the stability of entire nations, tightly gripping the throats of the less fortunate.

If you can sustain yourself without taking the life of another being, you honour nature's way. If not, then refrain from hunting and fishing for mere leisure, and avoid cruelty and abuse towards the animals you breed for your consumption.

All animals were once free until humans domesticated them. The power you hold over them should not be an excuse for mistreatment and torture.

I have seen the wickedness of greed as chickens and lambs are crammed in cages, deprived of their natural way of living, force-fed unnatural feed to expedite their growth and increase their yield. Reject such products from your tables.

Be mindful of the farmers who toil to grow the food you consume. Make certain they are not oppressed in their labour, for they should not starve while you pay their employers for their produce.

Eat local and eat fresh when you can, and refrain from foods that have been modified to defy nature.

Waste not, nor over-consume; for that is healthier for you and for the planet. When you have more food than you need on your table, do not throw any of it away. Find a person or an animal that needs to eat and give it to them instead.

If you eat a fruit, do not discard the seeds where they cannot grow; bury them instead, giving them the chance to sprout and grow. They might feed someone else one day."

"Tell us, Prophet! Can we still save our planet after all the damage it has suffered?" asked **Vadi**, the park's keeper.

The Prophet frowned before saying: "All the treasures left behind by past civilisations, all your art, science, and all your history may soon be swallowed by the rising tide. A tide that will not recede until it has drowned everything you know. That would mark the end of your story on this beautiful planet.

However, you should not worry about saving the planet, for the planet has the ability to heal itself once you have ceased your destructive actions. It has survived calamities worse than you can imagine, recovered, and thrived without any help.

What you should worry about instead, is saving your lives, the lives of your children and their children. You should be concerned *about preserving the entire history of human existence and the countless other creatures that share this planet with you.*

When I embarked on my journey all those years ago, I chose to walk on foot rather than taking buses, trains, or airplanes. And when I needed to take a boat to cross a sea, I always slept on its deck; drenched in sea water, washed by rain, with a face scorched by the sun and frozen by storms, and feet that were never dry.

I made this choice because even at a young age, I knew that I would never know what the earth is made of unless its elements consumed my body.

Above all, choosing to walk granted me countless encounters with nature, animals, and fellow humans that I would have missed otherwise.

When you consider the legacy you leave behind for your children, you should be deeply ashamed and more than alarmed. While you and your ancestors lived, they will be struggling to survive."

With a clear sense of helplessness, Vadi asked, "But why are the governments not doing more?"

"Because governments have short-sighted goals that they want to achieve, and would not choose the future over instant gains," the Prophet responded.

"But let me ask you: Are you, Vadi, doing more?" The Prophet then addressed the rest of the crowd: "Are each of you, the people, doing more?

Are you not buying more than you need? Are you not using plastic bags and containers, then discarding them in the oceans?

Are you not building larger than you need houses that require more energy to construct and maintain?

Are you not purchasing big cars and increasing air travel?

Are you not consuming excessive amounts of meat?

Are you not cutting down trees for mining, farming, or construction?

If the answer to any of these questions is yes, then you are as much to blame as the governments for the destruction of the planet and the future of humanity.

Each of you must take personal responsibility, starting at your own homes and workplaces.

Start conserving, preserving, recycling, and upcycling, then encourage your family, neighbours, and friends to do the same.

The water you save today ensures that your children will not die from thirst.

The clean air and oceans you preserve guarantee that your children will not gasp for breath.

Many species are going extinct as you stand here today, and it is not happening because of some cosmic incident; it is because of human greed and arrogance. Only when you are about to be consumed yourselves will you begin to worry."

The Prophet wiped a tear from her cheek.

Elsum, the banker of Herta, asked the Prophet about Money, Buying, and Selling.

The Prophet replied: "Money should have been one of the greatest inventions to facilitate human transactions. But alas, it has become a tool of oppression and the creator of classism.

Once, there was barter, where you exchanged what you had for what you needed. Then came banknotes and coins, pieces of printed paper or hammered metal claiming a worth beyond their intrinsic value, and serving as a medium of payment.

Later, plastic money in the form of cards emerged, declaring credit attributes but representing money that does not physically exist.

I do not blame those who need to borrow money to acquire what they require, but I abhor vendors who insist on credit payments.

These vendors collaborate with card issuers under the guise of facilitating transactions. In reality, they entice cardholders to purchase what they cannot afford, and in many cases, what you do not even need.

Later, through interest, fees, and penalties, you find yourselves indebted for much more than the initial purchase value. Upon sober reflection, you wonder how much of what you purchased you really needed and if it brought you real joy.

Consider what you truly gain from life as it nears its end, and you will likely find that you have accumulated far more than you ever needed. It is a lure of the capitalist system that encourages an absence of restraint and the pursuit of material possessions.

The media showcases individuals who have amassed great wealth and flaunts their lavish lifestyles. You see how they reside in grand houses, drive expensive cars, wear extravagant garments, and sail on boats or fly in private jets.

Yet, no one tells you how happy or content they genuinely are. You will not know if their homes are filled with love or not. You will not be told how many loyal friends those people have, the depth of their friendships, or the authenticity of their relationships.

A financially rich person often questions the intentions and motives of those who surround them like fruit flies swarm around a ripe peach. The rich would question whether these individuals seek genuine friendship and companionship or if they merely covet their wealth.

That, brothers and sisters, is a heavy cloud that can cast the darkest of shadows on the most intimate of liaisons.

But if you assume that by accumulating vast amounts of money, one attains contentment, then let me ask you, how much more can a person eat, and how many beds does one truly need? How many empty rooms in a mansion must the wealthy have before realising that emptiness and loneliness are their longest staying guests?

The idea of excess is repulsive in a world with diminishing resources, where people are starving and children lack education.

Understand this: Money hoarded solely for personal benefit is something you leave behind. Money spent for the betterment of others becomes your legacy."

"Then talk to us about Giving, good Prophet," said Mathel.

The Prophet spread her hands and said: "Giving is the act of repaying what the world has lent you during your lifetime. Whatever you possess, you cannot take with you after you die; it is only on loan to you as long as you are alive.

Consider the trees and learn from them, for they understand the true meaning of giving. After their fruits have been picked by people and animals, the trees do not hold onto the remaining fruits on their branches. They shed them onto the earth and stand bare, allowing new trees to grow. Over time, more trees emerge, creating an entire orchard, and the individual tree is no longer alone."

Aboram called out from a window, saying, "Sister, talk to us about Rulers and Laws."

The Prophet responded: "In ancient times, kings and queens claimed divine rights, or superior bloodlines to justify their rule over people they considered inferior. Many people believed them and followed them blindly, like a herd would a shepherd.

But people are not sheep.

As humanity evolves, so does morality. Many things that your ancestors accepted and endured are now deemed unthinkable. With the growth of humanity comes a growth of morality.

Who among you can condone slavery today when, just decades ago, it was widely accepted in many nations?

Why do you continue to accept being ruled when you can all live as equal beings, building civilisations and fulfilling your aspirations through respect and decency?

Given the opportunity, people can manage their own affairs by themselves. They understand their aspirations and what they and their children need. They can organise the human relationships necessary to create a fair and fruitful life.

Many laws were imposed by a select few who assumed they knew better than everyone else. These individuals, with access to power, whether through money, media, or arms, crafted constitutions that decades and centuries later still serve the interest of the few who created them and their successors.

How many people are aware of, let alone have a say in, the constitution of the countries they live in now?

Every human being has the right to be heard. The collective should serve the individual, as it is the individuals who form the collective.

Those entrusted to serve the individual or the collective should not be seen or treated anything other than that: servants to the individual and the collective.

Unfortunately, power and greed often transform the supposed servants into tyrants, and ignorance makes those who should be served easy prey.

The tyrants would soon set up various establishments and house them in grand buildings that dwarf you into accepting their superiority over you, and admitting your own inferiority to them.

They make laws and organise periodic elections in different regions to deceive you into thinking that your vote matters. Yet, upon closer examination, you realise that these divisions were designed to maintain the tyrants in power and enable them to pass on their rule to other tyrants who will continue to serve their own interests.

They monitor your actions and eavesdrop on your words, using any available technology to maintain control over your lives.

No one should be allowed to rule over another. If we believe in the equality of all *human beings, then we should behave accordingly. Individuals contribute to the collective, and the collective serves and embraces each individual.*

Throughout centuries and millennia, rulers have employed various systems to ensure your compliance and obedience; from nationalism to capitalism, from socialism to communism, and more.

They designed orders that ruled over you, calling them democracies, bureaucracies, autocracies, monarchies, republics, and many. Yet, never have "Humanity" and "Equality" been the guiding principles of governance.

Humanity and Equality teach you that others are as important as you are, regardless of their colour, wealth, language, or religion.

Humanity and Equality emphasise the importance of schools, hospitals, and children's playgrounds over cathedrals and palaces. They demonstrate that if money were spent on housing and equal opportunities, there would be no need for penitentiaries.

They can teach tolerance and love, ultimately eliminating the need for armies and wars. Most importantly, they will lead you to believe that no human being should feel lesser than their true worth."

The clear voice of **Vera** came forth from a balcony down an alley, "Tell us about Freedom, Sister Prophet."

The Prophet spoke: "You are all existing on this earth not because you freely chose to exist, but as a product of someone else's choice and circumstance.

Your parents and their peers, driven by their ego and self-preservation, conceive you, assign names to you and incorporate you into the religion that they follow.

You grow up defined by a name, a race, a religion, and a nationality that you did not choose for yourself.

If later in life you are unhappy with these choices, it will be difficult, if not impossible, to change them due to social and political constraints.

If you, as human beings, did not have a choice in your existence, you should, at least, have the freedom to choose how you live that existence.

Freedom is the means to change your being from an object to a subject. It is your birthright, and it comes with responsibilities.

Your right to choose may sometimes collide with someone else's similar right. It is at those times that you must seek a social agreement based on human decency, equality, and fairness to preserve your freedoms.

Let no one tell you that you are free because of them. You are free because it is your inherent right to be free. However, you must earn the preservation of your freedom.

I ache for a world where people can choose their own names, and where individuals select their beliefs. A world where people do not need boundaries, nationalities, or passports to prove themselves to anyone.

Above all, I long for a world where people are not ostracised or incarcerated because of their colour, religion, or opinions.

Countless times, have I envied birds flying freely over the borders of countries. From above, they watch humans being stopped at fortified crossings erected by other humans. They see people forced to prove their identities and justify their purpose for crossing those invisible lines. The birds fly in flocks without needing to authenticate themselves, or explaining the motive behind their migration to anyone.

Nations have shed seas of blood to establish and defend those invisible lines. They have sacrificed many of their children to protect the sovereignty of their borders.

Let me ask you though, how sovereign are you within a cage? What are your rulers afraid of? Why be confined within boundaries when the entire world is open to explore and embrace?

Governments and rulers claim to protect your freedom, defending you from those who may infringe upon your belongings, language, beliefs, and way of life. They impose restrictions, arguing that they preserve your uniqueness in the world.

They quarrel and clash with others over imaginary lines on land and in the sea, even claiming ownership of the heavens above both.

I ask those governments and rulers: Where would your knowledge be without the wisdom that travelled to you from the far corners of the world?

How many words from other languages enrich your own? How unique are your genes to your claimed race?

And indeed, has your current religion not been something else once?

Brothers and sisters, always strive to fulfil your right to be free; free in your deeds and free in your thoughts. Advocate for this right, fight for it when necessary, and defend the rights of others in their pursuit of freedom.

Every person has a story to tell, and no one has the right to silence that story."

Herta's priest, **Dari,** stepped forward and asked the prophet about Faith and Religion.

The prophet said: "Faith is the craving of your heart and mind to find the meaning of your existence. It tries to find explanations to the universe and its phenomena until science can. It is a useful instrument for your serenity and inner peace.

Religion, on the other hand, is an institution and often an industry. It regiments thoughts and chips away at your humanity; for is it not you and other priests, brother Dari, who preach that yours is the righteous path while other religions stray?

You have witnessed apparently devout individuals committing hurtful deeds, and others who have never entered a temple refuse to harm a soul. Yet, you and your fellow priests claim that Religion is the sole source of morality.

It was because of the institution of Religion, and not because of Faith itself, that blood was shed throughout history. Yet, that hasn't stopped the perpetrators from claiming that theirs is a religion of tolerance, peace, and compassion.

While Faith yearns for reason, Religion implores you not to question.

Priests will tell you that some things are beyond your comprehension when your inquiry surpasses their knowledge.

And when you wonder why your prayers go unanswered, they will blame you for some hidden impurity in your heart.

Rulers understand the power of Faith and use Religion to mobilise you under the guise of protecting and spreading the "Truth". They will tell you that your beliefs are threatened by others and must be fought for.

You, the people of Herta and the world, may believe in a god or not. That is your soul's peace, not anyone else's.

Your place in the universe is to make this short journey of your lives useful to others and meaningful for yourselves.

Love nature and all living things within it to find serenity in your hearts.

Refrain from doing unto others what you would not want done unto you and your loved ones.

Listen to the stories of your fellow humans and empathise with them.

Refuse to take what is not rightfully yours, and rise above greed.

Free your mind from grudges and judgments.

Reach out and help an orphaned child or a hungry person, relieve an animal from abuse, and water a thirsty tree.

Keep the planet clean and refrain from polluting it.

If you can do all that, then your purpose for being is fulfilled, and you will have achieved godliness.

You will also know the answers to all that you have asked me and more; you will never need to wait for another prophet."

The Prophet raised her right hand and said: "Let me be now, brothers and sisters, for much has been said and the sun is setting on the day.

Go to your homes and to your loved ones, reflect upon what I have said, and take from it that which fills your heart."

Dari, the priest, smiled at the Prophet with teary eyes, took off his mantle, threw it onto the ground, and walked away with the rest of the crowd.

The Prophet then sat down cross-legged. She spread her arms and rested her hands on her knees. With her eyes closed, she turned her palms upward. On her right palm was the birthmark in the shape of a star.

When the sun rose on the following day, the Prophet was gone, and her house had been knocked down. No one knew if the Prophet had done it, or if the house was waiting to see her one last time before surrendering to its age.

As people walked through the rubble, they heard the distant voice of the Prophet singing:

"I built my home on trust and love,

With a window as wide open as the sky above.

May the wind come and rest among the things that we share,

May we float atop an ocean, and may it take us everywhere."